WORLD OF SPORTS

ROCK CLIMBING

Published by Smart Apple Media
123 South Broad Street, Mankato, Minnesota 56001

Photography: pages 7, 12, 18, 19, 21—CORBIS/Galen Rowell;
page 13—CORBIS/Jon Sparks; page 23—CORBIS/Paul A.
Sonders; page 28—CORBIS/Jay Syverson

Design and Production by EvansDay Design
Editorial assistance by Catherine J. Bernardy

LIBRARY OF CONGRESS CATALOGING-IN-PUBLICATION DATA

Ryan, Pat.
Rock climbing / by Pat Ryan.
p. cm. — (World of sports)
Includes index.
Summary: Details the history, equipment, techniques,
and competitions of rock climbing.
ISBN 1-887068-57-0
1. Rock climbing—Juvenile literature. [1. Rock climbing.]
I. Title. II. Series: World of sports (Mankato, Minn.)
GV200.2.B49 2000
796.52'23—dc21 98-33683

9 8 7 6 5 4 3 2

PAT RYAN

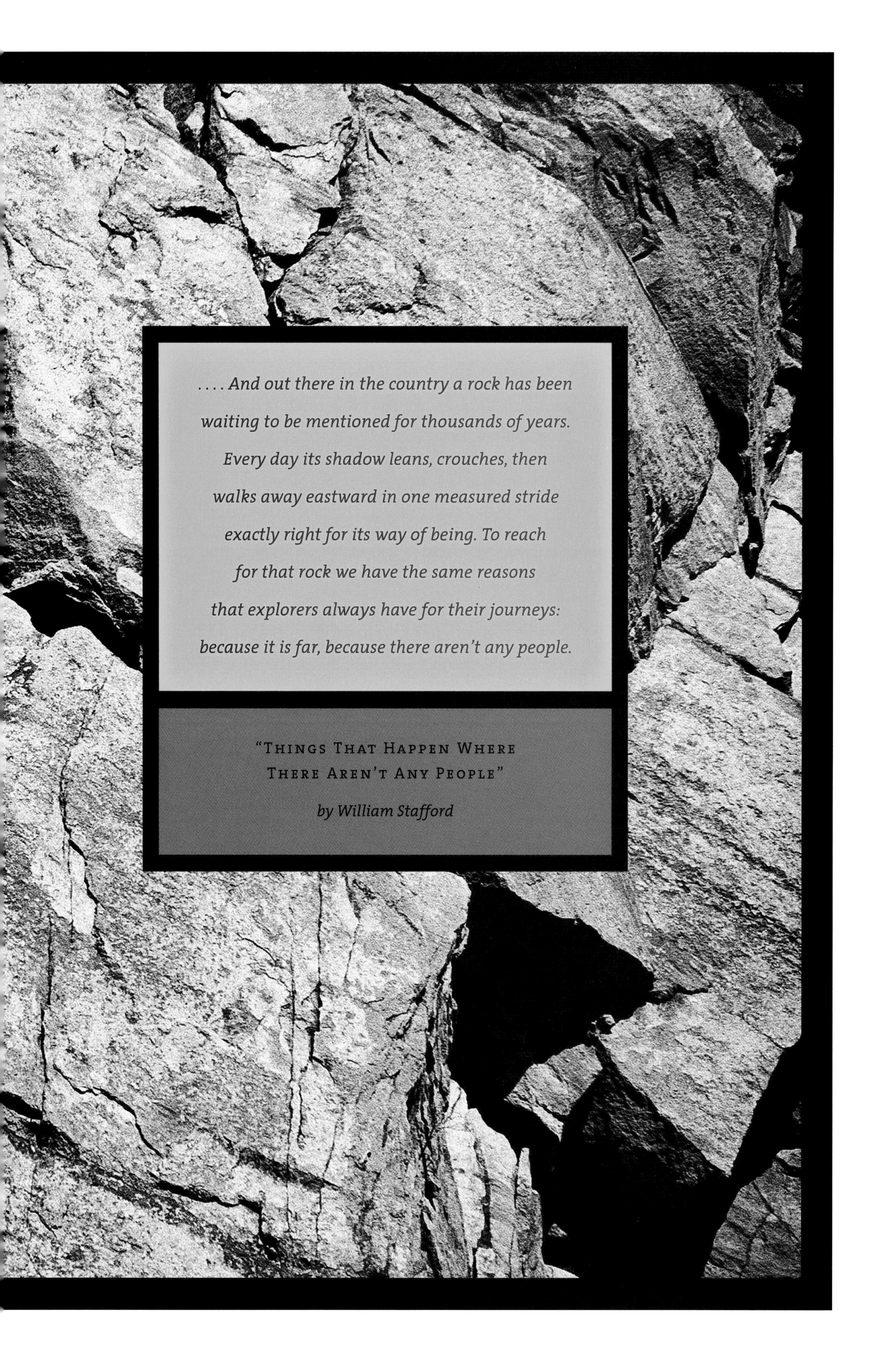
. . . . And out there in the country a rock has been
waiting to be mentioned for thousands of years.
Every day its shadow leans, crouches, then
walks away eastward in one measured stride
exactly right for its way of being. To reach
for that rock we have the same reasons
that explorers always have for their journeys:
because it is far, because there aren't any people.
"Things That Happen Where
There Aren't Any People"
by William Stafford

Young Champions

KATIE BROWN LOOKS like a spider as she scales the 42-foot (12.8 m) wall at the X Games at Newport, Rhode Island. She hangs effortlessly from overhangs and steadily works her way up the face of the wall. With only 60 seconds of her allotted eight minutes remaining, Brown reaches the point where French climber Laurence Guyon and European Champion Liv Sansoz fell. But she has more than enough time. At the finish line, Brown calmly swings into position for the final handhold and pulls herself up. She is the only woman to complete the climb on the wall in the difficulty trial. She smiles. "It was a hard climb," she tells a reporter.

According to Dakota legend, Devil's Tower in Wyoming was created when a bear attacked girls who were playing by a stream. The girls took shelter on the highest rock they could find and pleaded with the Spirits for help. The rock grew taller to keep the girls safe, but the bear also grew and clawed long, vertical furrows in the rock face out of frustration.

Youth is no barrier when it comes to being a champion rock climber. At age 15, Brown took the big prize at ESPN's X Games in 1996. The five-foot (1.5 m), 85-pound (39 kg) climber "doesn't realize how good she is,

Few sports are as physically demanding as rock climbing, which helps to build total-body strength and endurance.

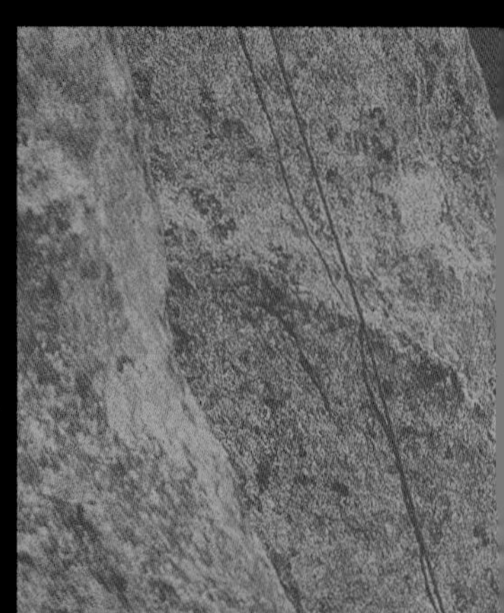

and I don't think she wants to realize it," her mother Eileen Brown said. "When she started climbing, I don't think she imagined it would lead to a gold medal." By 1998, Brown had won three consecutive gold medals at the X Games.

Brown became the women's national champion in 1996 after winning all five of the year's national competitions. She participated on the 1997 U.S. Climbing Team, comprised of the top 10 men and women climbers in the country. The top

leg *a part or stage of a race*

redpoint *to achieve a climb—without falling or retreating—after many tries at the route; as opposed to an onsight climb*

onsight climbs *climbs completed successfully on the first attempt without falling or retreating; as opposed to a redpoint climb*

ALTHOUGH CLIMBING COMPETITIONS ARE BECOMING POPULAR EVENTS, MOST CLIMBERS COMPETE ONLY AGAINST THEMSELVES—AND THE WALL OF ROCK.

four scores from the national and continental championships determine the selection of team members, who then compete worldwide in the annual World Cup. Brown has also taken first place at an Italian competition that is considered one of the most prestigious in Europe.

One of her teenage cohorts, 1996 men's champion Chris Sharma, became the youngest competitor ever to win a **leg** of climbing's World Cup in 1997. That same year, he became the first American to climb a 130-foot (39.6 m) section of volcanic rock in Smith Rock State Park in Oregon, one of the most difficult climbs in the United States.

Tommy Caldwell has quickly become one of the best redpoint climbers in the United States. In January 1998, at the age of 19, he became the third American (and the sixth climber) to **redpoint** a tremendously difficult climb at Smith Rock called "Just Do It." It took seven tries over a period of three days to complete the route, which is considered America's third-hardest climb. "It was a lot easier than I thought it was going to be," Caldwell said later. "I had really psyched myself up to do it, and when I got there, I was surprised how fast it went."

Mount Edith Cavell in the Canadian Rockies was named after a British nurse who was falsely accused by the Germans of spying during World War I.

James Lintz is another accomplished young climber. By the age of 19, Lintz had already completed some of the most difficult **onsight climbs** on the East Coast.

Centuries of Challenge

MANY EXPERTS BELIEVE that the art of climbing is a relatively recent development. The first people to climb rocks for the sheer sport of it were French mountaineers. In the late 18th century, young Genevese professor Horace Bénédict de Saussure became fascinated by France's Mount Blanc. At 15,782 feet (4,810 m), Mount Blanc is the highest peak in the Alps. De Saussure offered a reward to the first person who successfully climbed the mountain.

In 1998, Venezuelan José Pereyra established a free-climbing route in southern Utah, possibly the hardest pure crack line in America. He named the 100-foot (30.5 m) climb "No Way José."

A few brave souls set off to grab the prize but never returned, becoming the first fatalities of mountaineering. Finally, in 1786, Dr. Michel Paccard and his guide Jacques Balmat raised the French flag atop the mountain. The word of their quest spread throughout Europe and the world. The age of modern climbing had begun.

Mount Everest in the Himalayan Mountains is the highest peak in the world. Its summit scratches the clouds at an altitude of 29,028 feet

Mount Everest, which rises nearly six miles (9.6 km) into the sky, offers mountaineers the most challenging and spectacular climb in the world.

(8,848 m). A British team was the first to make the difficult, dangerous trek to the Asian summit in 1953. The climb took 47 days—from April 13 to May 29. Mountaineer Edmund Hillary, a New Zealand native, was the first team member to reach the peak.

"A few more whacks of the ice-axe in the firm snow and we stood on the top," Hillary wrote. "My initial feelings were

big wall *a rock face 1,000 feet (305 m) high or higher that requires a climber to spend at least one night on the climb in order to reach the top*

monolith *a gigantic object, such as a huge rock face*

Unlike the snug, light shoes worn by rock climbers, mountaineering boots are heavy shoes equipped with long cleats for gripping icy slopes.

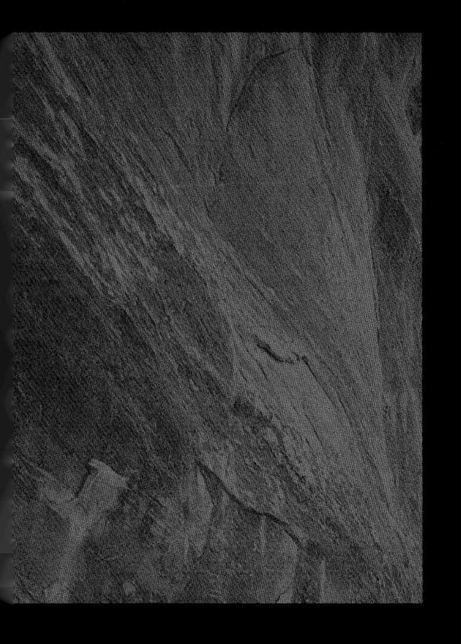

of relief—relief that there were no more steps to cut, no more ridges to traverse and no more humps to tantalize us with hopes of success. I looked at Tenzing [Norgay, a Sherpa] and in spite of the balaclava, goggles, and oxygen mask all encrusted with long icicles that concealed his face, there was no disguising his infectious grin of pure delight as he looked around him."

Mark Bowling, founder of Joshua Tree Rock Climbing School, tied the record for the most climbs in California's Joshua Tree National Park. Bowling free-soloed 200 climbs in 18 hours.

But whether on Mount Everest or a boulder, climbing is in the challenge—not the height. When the climbing community first started rating the difficulty of climbing routes, a **big wall** of granite called El Capitán in Yosemite National Park was considered the most difficult sport climb in the world. Climbers had generally avoided the 2,900-foot (884 m) **monolith**, noting the abundance of blank sections where there were no useful cracks or handholds.

In 1958, the first team began scaling the wall. By the 11th day of their ascent, the men had been on the rock face more than twice as long as any American team on a climb. Altogether, including the time needed to plan the route, the climb took 45 days of muscle-wrenching effort. But it ushered in a new era of North American rock climbing.

"It was not at all clear to me who was conqueror and who was conquered," Warren Harding, a member of the team, said later. "I do recall that El Cap seemed to be in much better condition than I was."

There's More Than One Way to Climb a Rock

ROCK CLIMBERS FIND joy in scaling rock faces such as El Capitán, Devil's Tower in Wyoming, the Shawangunks in New York, or any of thousands of ridges and bluffs across North America and around the world. They cling to cliffs with nothing but hundreds of feet of air between them and solid ground. Their bloody, taped-up fingers grip knobs the size of a child's fist, and they wedge their toes into cracks the width of a book's spine. They propel themselves upward using ropes, safety harnesses, a partner to **belay** them, metal devices that they cram into rock faces, and **carabiners** to guide their ropes.

In 1998, Steve Gerberding, a member of the official North Face Climbing Team, co-held the record for the most ascents of El Capitán. He made 74 ascents, including three ascents via routes that had never been climbed before.

It's not a sport for the timid. Climbers must leave their doubts and fears at the bottom of the route, because the task they have chosen takes all of their concentration, flexibility, and strength. Climbing pushes them to the limits of their physical and mental abilities.

The pleasure of simple climbs leads many novices to take rock climbing classes, which are offered at universities, sports stores, and athletic clubs. There are at least 400 indoor rock climbing walls in the United States. New climbers typically train on these walls, learning important skills and techniques.

In 1998, Spaniard Josune Bereziartu became the first woman to redpoint a 5.14b route. She worked for three years to perfect her ascent on the climb "Honky Tonky," located at a crag called Oñate.

Bouldering also helps beginners to learn to balance themselves on handholds and footholds. This type of climbing is called **free climbing**. In free climbing, handholds and toeholds are provided only by the rock. Climbers use equipment for safety purposes, but not to help them move up the rock face.

belay *to secure a climber*

carabiners *metal rings used to guide a climber's safety rope*

bouldering *climbing on boulders; also, climbing at the foot of a route to a height where it is still safe to jump off*

free climbing *climbing using only natural holds; as opposed to aid climbing*

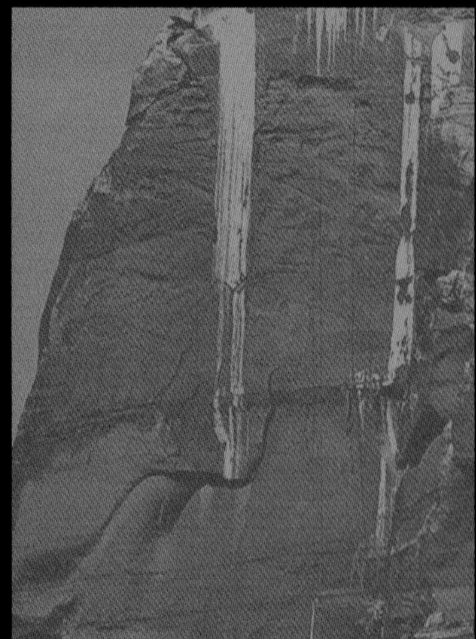

A SECURELY ANCHORED ROPE IS PERHAPS A CLIMBER'S MOST IMPORTANT PIECE OF SAFETY EQUIPMENT. IT CAN PREVENT A SLIP FROM BECOMING A DEADLY FALL.

No matter what type of climbing a person chooses to do, balance, concentration, and strength are critical in getting to the top.

Enthusiasts can choose between **top-roping**, sport climbing, soloing, and traditional climbing. Top-roping is done in controlled conditions, usually with the safety of a pre-placed **anchor** and knowledge of the course before the climb begins. These precautions don't eliminate short falls, but a person called a **belayer** is attached to the other end of a climber's rope. The belayer watches throughout the climb and attempts to prevent problems. He or she continually monitors the rope to ensure that slack remains at a minimum. Slack must be taken up before a falling person can be stopped. Belay devices attached to the ropes add **friction** to stop a fall if a climber should slip.

top-roping *a method of climbing in which a rope anchored at the top of the route always holds the climber; as opposed to lead climbing*

anchor *a tree or other immobile object at the top of a climb; also, any point where the rope is fixed to the rock*

Sport climbing involves tackling routes of gymnastic difficulty. Sport climbers must be able to perform stretches and odd pivots, and they must have a keen sense of balance.

Soloing simply means climbing alone. Soloing without any climbing aids is called free soloing. Free soloists use equipment only for protection. Traditional climbing comes from the mountaineering traditions of Europe and Asia. It includes ice climbing—ascending snow, glaciers, frozen waterfalls, and even huge icicle overhangs.

In **lead climbing**, a leader and a follower ascend together a **pitch** at a time. The leader is the more experienced climber, so he or she establishes the path taken by both climbers. Teams can traverse more routes with this method than with top-roping, but it is a little more dangerous. The

In 1996, Erik Weihenmeyer climbed the sheer, vertical face of El Capitán. He has been blind since the age of 13.

EXPERIENCED ROCK CLIMBERS KNOW HOW TO COMBINE STRATEGY, FLEXIBILITY, AND THE USE OF CLIMBING AIDS FOR A SUCCESSFUL ASCENT.

belayer *a person attached to the climber via a rope who attempts to stop falls and guide the climber*

friction *a resistance that occurs when two surfaces rub together*

lead climbing *a technique in which an experienced climber ascends ahead of a second climber; as opposed to top-roping*

pitch *in lead climbing, a section of an ascent shorter than the length of rope being used by the climbers; typically 150 feet (45.7 m)*

chocks *metal wedging devices crammed into cracks; also called protection*

route must contain areas where a belayer can be secure, and the rock must provide many cracks where climbers can secure the rope with aids, or "protection," such as **chocks**, bolts, or other cramming or wedging devices. Climbers push these devices into cracks in the rock and clip their ropes to them with carabiners. In some cases, they must drill into the rock in order to secure their safety devices.

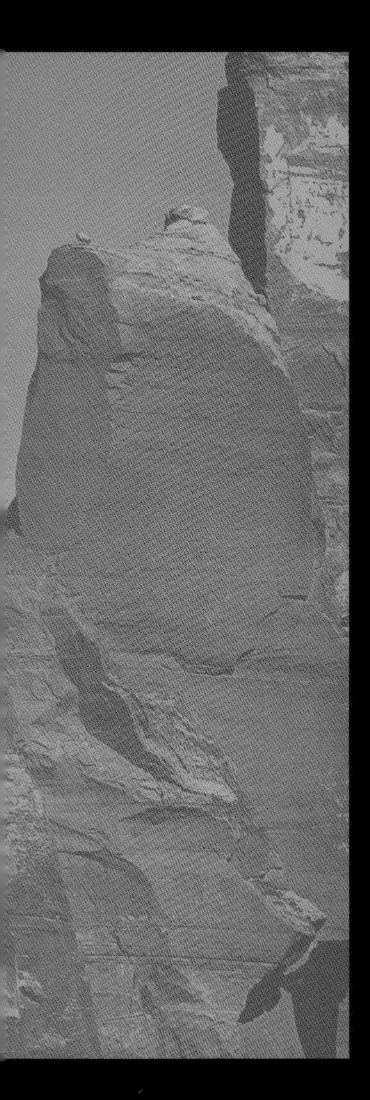

Chocks crammed into crevices are sometimes the only way that climbers can find a solid handhold or rope anchor.

The Importance of Protection

WHEN A PERSON'S LIFE involves hanging from vertical bluffs and cliffs hundreds of feet in the air, searching for cracks and knobs of rock, proper safety equipment is paramount. Footwear is basic but important. Rock climbers get most of their body support from footholds and leg strength. Climbers can only hang by their fingers for so long before **sewing machine arm** sets in.

The first ascent of Devil's Tower was made on July 4, 1893, with artificial means. Climbers William Rogers and Willard Ripley used a crude ladder of oak, ash, and willow pegs, driving them into a continuous 350-foot (107 m) crack on the monolith's south side.

Unlike mountaineering boots, rock climbing shoes don't need to provide warmth. Instead, they must provide as great a surface area as possible and be highly flexible, so climbers can wedge their feet into narrow cracks. Some modern climbing shoes have a sole made of sticky rubber to provide better grip.

Climbers must also protect their heads. Helmets, sometimes called "brain buckets," provide protection in case of a fall. More importantly, they deflect falling rocks and debris.

AFTER REACHING THE TOP OF THE ROCK FACE, A CLIMBER MAY SECURE A STRONG ROPE TO HIS OR HER HARNESS FOR A MORE LEISURELY DESCENT BACK TO THE BOTTOM.

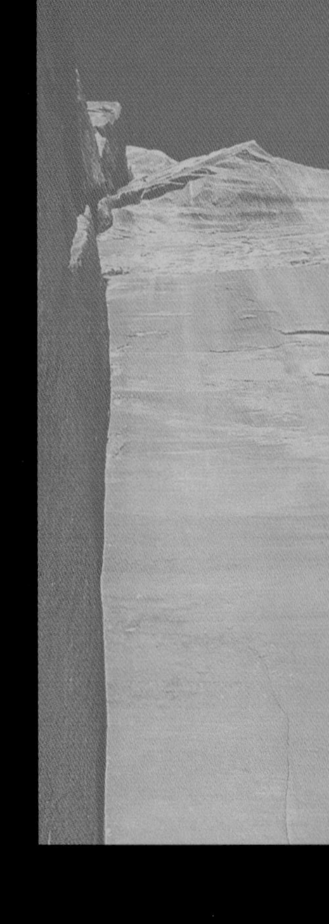

Climbing aids, starting with ropes, are also safety equipment. Today's ropes offer resiliency and shock absorption, much like a bungee cord. Climbing with safety ropes requires a harness. Padded nylon harnesses wrap around a climber's waist and include loops to support the climber's legs. Harnesses also come equipped with a belay plate, which helps provide the rope friction necessary to stop a falling climber.

Rope flows through carabiners to keep it from rubbing on the rock face and fraying. Carabiners also connect rope to

sewing machine arm *the involuntary shaking of a stressed muscle*

rappelling *to descend a rock face by sliding down a rope*

STRONG AND RELIABLE CARABINERS ARE OF UTMOST IMPORTANCE TO CLIMBERS. THEY KEEP ROPES FROM BINDING OR FRAYING, MAKING FOR A SMOOTHER AND SAFER CLIMB.

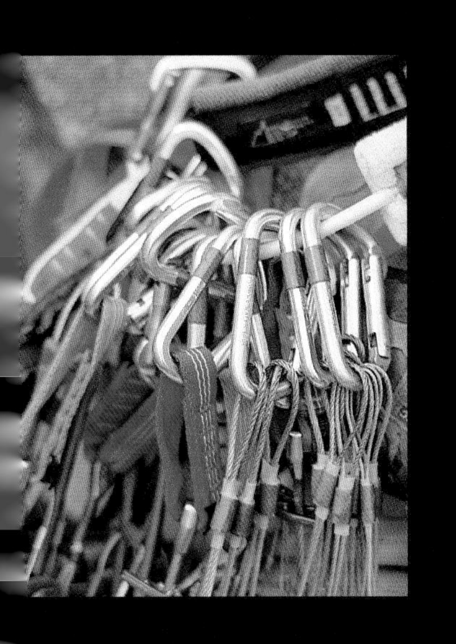

climbing aids that are jammed into cracks. Rock climbers often insert these aids along a route to shorten the length of a fall. A rope enters a carabiner through a spring-locked gate; the gate opens like a safety pin.

On the first climb of the North Ridge of the Grand Teton Glacier in 1931, Fritiof Fryxell's gear had not arrived in camp. As a result, he was forced to pioneer the climb wearing a pair of mismatched work boots.

The original carabiners, or "biners," were oval. Today, many are D-shaped to provide better protection. As an extra precaution, climbers often clip ropes with two carabiners positioned so their gates oppose each other. Climbers use carabiners continually in climbing and **rappelling**. Some steep overhangs do not allow climbers to rappel, so they must climb backward, or downclimb.

The typical climber's pouch also contains chocks and descenders. Chocks include wedges and cams. These devices use spring releases to provide secure anchor in rock-face cracks. True to their name, descenders include all the tools that help climbers get down cliffs. The most common descender is the figure eight, a small metal device that creates friction to control the flow of the rope so a person doesn't descend too quickly or lose control of the rope.

North America's first significant mountain climb took place in 1820, when three men ascended the 14,110-foot (4,301 m) Pikes Peak near what is now Colorado Springs.

Climbers also carry chalk bags to help them maintain firm handholds. Like gymnasts on parallel bars, climbers must keep their hands dry. Slippery fingers are dangerous.

Although a safety harness and helmet are important accessories of the sport, there is no substitute for careful planning and footwork.

Skilled climbers can find firm footing and handholds on even the most vertical walls of rock.

Climbers must carry anything else they will need during a trip—a list of supplies that can include sleeping bags or mattresses, water, dehydrated food, and a tiny cookstove. But monoliths such as El Capitán offer no ledges where climbers can set up camp. In these situations, climbers sleep while dangling in mid-air, stuffed into sleeping bags that resemble cocoons.

Because It's There

CLIMBING HAS INCREASED in popularity over the past few decades. Better regulations, improved equipment, the creation of indoor climbing walls, and a new climber's code of safety have all made the sport safer and more fun. As a result, more people are willing to try it.

Some people think that rock climbing will become the next popular fitness craze. As a total-body exercise, the sport works all muscles and improves a person's coordination, balance, and flexibility. "I've competed in a lot of sports," said professional sport climber Shelley Presson, "but this is the most kickingest sport there is for staying in shape. I'll go to the grocery store and people will see my arms and ask what I do to stay in shape. 'Do you work out a lot?' No, I rock climb."

Climber John Mattson of Flagstaff, Arizona, has established many hard crack lines at the Flagstaff crag Paradise Forks, some of which remained unrepeated as of 1999. Some of his routes are in the 5.13a-b levels.

Some industrious climbers build their own climbing walls. A room and sheets of plywood with holds attached to them can become a

training station. Some climbers host competitions on their own courses. They hold timed climbs or play a game called "Add On." In this game, one climber does a routine, and the next climber repeats the same sequence but adds a new move.

Indoor facilities build an athlete's confidence and strength so that he or she can perform in the great outdoors. Beginners usually start out by exploring local areas for challenging sites. After finishing these climbs, they may move on to tougher routes throughout a region or state.

Magazine articles and guidebooks list pages and pages of climbs and often include detailed route descriptions and ratings that indicate the difficulty of each climb. Most sources rely on the Sierra Club System for ratings. Under this system,

INDOOR CLIMBING WALLS ALLOW NOVICES TO LEARN THE BASICS OF ROCK CLIMBING AND GIVE EXPERTS A PLACE FOR COMPETITIONS.

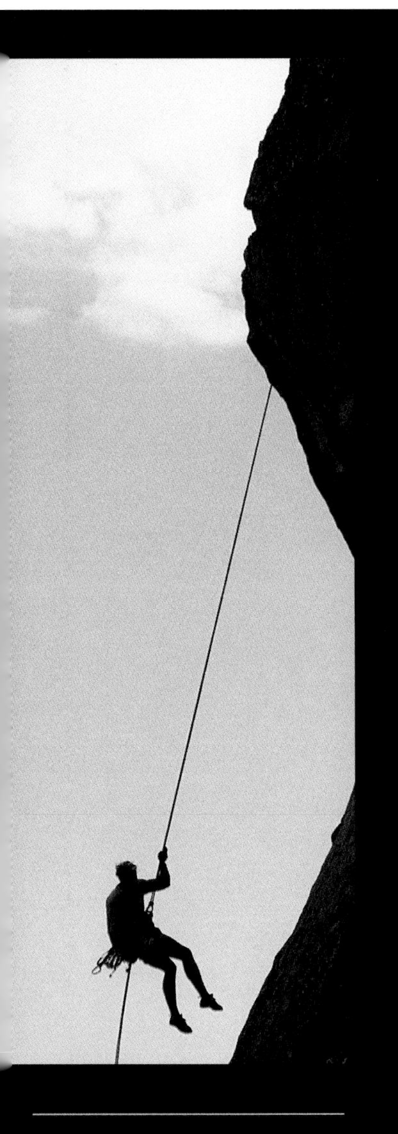

Blue skies, fresh air, and the solitude of the climb are just a few of the reasons that more and more people are taking up the sport of climbing.

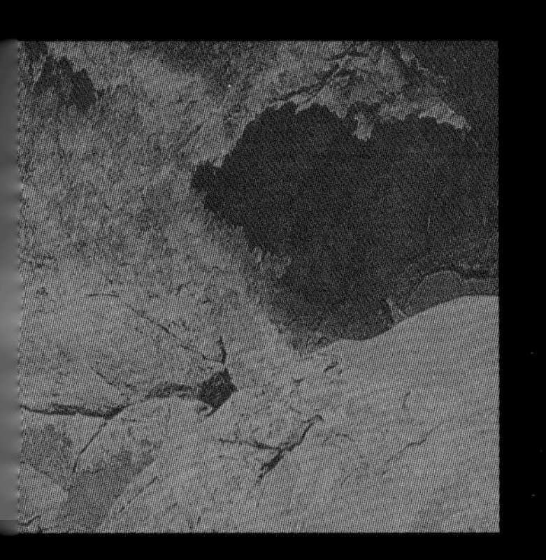

class one and class two climbs are low-exertion walking and hiking paths. Class three climbs require handholds and footholds. Class four routes involve steep climbs where ropes and other equipment are needed.

Class five climbs are the steep inclines that only experienced rock climbers tackle. These areas are divided into 15 categories of increasing difficulty, ranging from 5.0 to 5.14. The most difficult routes are further distinguished with letters *a* through *d*. The highest rating any climb can receive is a 5.14d.

The American Sport Climbers Federation (ASCF) governs climbing contests throughout the United States. The organization works with contest sponsors, establishes contest rules, selects courses, and ranks athletes throughout the nation. Contests are held on local, regional, and national levels. Climbers compete in both speed and difficulty events, with men and women competing in separate divisions. To compete at a national competition, women must be able to traverse a 5.11d, and men a 5.12a. The ASCF also oversees junior climbers and their competitions.

Climbing can be done anywhere, but the western United States offers a wealth of spectacular areas, including the Rocky Mountains. The awesome beauty of these mountains and the Canadian Rockies makes North America a climber's playground. Elsewhere,

Dan Osman, a rock climber who deliberately falls from all kinds of climbs, is designing and improving climbing aids, belaying equipment, and techniques to improve climbers' safety during falls. As of 1999, he held the record for the longest free-fall from a standing structure, a 660-foot (200 m) drop from a bridge in California.

the Needles area in South Dakota's Black Hills provides midwesterners with a challenge. Residents of the eastern portion of the United States can climb the Shawangunk Range in New York.

In June 1998, the United States Forest Service banned many of the kinds of safety equipment used in **aid climbing**—such as bolts and **pitons**—from wilderness areas, because such equipment becomes a permanent part of the rock face. The ban affected such world-famous climbing areas as Mt. Whitney, Tahquitz Rock, and Suicide Rock in California; the Cirque of Towers in Wyoming's Wind River Range; Lone Peak Cirque in Utah; the Elephant's Perch in Idaho; and Prussik Peak and the Snow Creek Wall in Washington's Cascades.

Climbing is still allowed at these locations. However, without the use of equipment, many routes may no longer be safe to climb. Officials have also closed much of Hueco Tanks State Historical Park in Texas to climbing in order to protect Native American rock art and other archaeological sites.

Fortunately, climbers will never face a shortage of climbs. Challenges are literally as numerous as boulders. Whether they're climbing a backyard bluff or a mountain that's half a world away from home, climbers find new ways of improv-

In May 1998, American Tom Whittaker became the first disabled person to ascend Mount Everest. He made it to the top on his second try that month. Whittaker, who wears an artificial leg below his right knee, first attempted the peak in 1995 and failed about 1,800 feet (549 m) below the summit.

aid climbing *ascending a route with the use of equipment; as opposed to free climbing*

pitons *metal spikes that can be hammered into a crack*

NORTH AMERICA'S MANY RUGGED WILDERNESS AREAS OFFER CLIMBERS OF ALL SKILL LEVELS CHALLENGING ROUTES AND STUNNING SCENERY.

THE SPORT OF CLIMBING HAS EXPLODED IN POPULARITY IN THE LAST DECADE. THE CHALLENGE OF THE CLIMB CALLS MANY ATHLETES BACK AGAIN AND AGAIN.

ing their abilities. They develop both physical and mental strength, and this strength leads to greater accomplishments.

Serious climbers are not discouraged by routes that seem impossible. If it's vertical, they're likely to climb it, no matter how difficult the climb. Why? There are as many explanations as there are climbers. However, the classic answer was given by a climber many decades ago: because it's there. Just because it hasn't been done doesn't mean that it can't.

INDEX

A
American Sport Climbers Federation (ASCF) 29–30

B
Balmat, Jacques 10
Bereziartu, Josune 16
Black Hills 30
Bowling, Mark 13
Brown, Katie 6, 8–9

C
Caldwell, Tommy 9
Cascades 30
Cirque of Towers 30
climbing
 gear 20, 22–25
 history 10
 safety equipment 20, 22–23, 30
 types 9, 10, 13, 16–19, 30
  aid 30
  bouldering 16
  free 10, 13, 16–17
  lead 18–19
  onsight 9
  redpoint 9
  soloing 17, 18
  sport 17, 18
  top-roping 17, 18
  traditional 17
 walls 26, 28

D
de Saussure, Horace Bénédict 10
Devil's Tower 6, 14, 20

E
El Capitán 13, 14, 18, 25
Elephant's Perch 30

F
Fryxell, Fritiof 23

G
Gerberding, Steve 14
Grand Teton Glacier 23
Guyon, Laurence 6

H
Harding, Warren 13
Hillary, Edmund 12–13
Himalayan Mountains 10, 12–13
"Honky Tonky" 16
Hueco Tanks State Historical Park 30

J
Joshua Tree National Park 13
Joshua Tree Rock Climbing School 13
"Just Do It" 9

L
Lintz, James 9
Lone Peak Cirque 30

M
Mattson, John 26
Mount Blanc 10
Mount Edith Cavell 9
Mount Everest 10, 12–13, 30
Mt. Whitney 30

N
"No Way José" 10
North Face Climbing Team 14

O
Oñate 16
Osman, Dan 29

P
Paccard, Michel 10
Paradise Forks 26
Pereyra, José 10
Pikes Peak 24
Presson, Shelley 26
Prussik Peak 30

R
rappelling 22, 23
Ripley, Willard 20
Rocky Mountains 29
Rogers, William 20

S
Sansoz, Liv 6
Sharma, Chris 9
Shawangunk Range 14, 30
Sierra Club System 28–29
Smith Rock State Park 9
Snow Creek Wall 30
Stafford, William 5
Suicide Rock 30

T
Tahquitz Rock 30
"Things That Happen Where There Aren't Any People" 5

U
U.S. Climbing Team 8
United States Forest Service 30

W
Weihenmeyer, Erik 18
Whittaker, Tom 30
Wind River Range 30
World Cup 9

X
X Games 6, 8

Y
Yosemite National Park 13